The Legend of Michigan

By Trinka Hakes Noble

Illustrated by Gijsbert van Frankenhuyzen

I believe we stand on the shoulders of our ancestors. This book is dedicated to my American ancestors; those who arrived in New England in 1645, and my Native American ancestors who were already here.

With my deepest respect,

THN

Many thanks to Sieffre Smalley, for wrapping himself in animal furs and pretending to be cold in 65 degree temperatures. You made a great "young warrior." Your acting was superb and your ready smile was a bonus. And thanks to our entomologist friend and neighbor, Walter Pett, who was my "old warrior" in the story. I know it's not quite a modeling gig but you were a natural. It was fun watching you and Sieffre talking "bugs."

Gijsbert

———

Text Copyright © 2006 Trinka Hakes Noble
Illustration Copyright © 2006 Gijsbert van Frankenhuyzen

All rights reserved. No part of this book may be reproduced in any manner without the express written consent of the publisher, except in the case of brief excerpts in critical reviews and articles. All inquiries should be addressed to:

Sleeping Bear Press™
310 North Main Street, Suite 300
Chelsea, MI 48118
www.sleepingbearpress.com

© 2006 Thomson Gale, a part of the Thomson Corporation.

Thomson, Star Logo and Sleeping Bear Press are trademarks and Gale is a registered trademark used herein under license.

Printed and bound in Canada

10 9 8 7 6 5 4 3 2 1

Library of Congress Cataloging-in-Publication Data

Noble, Trinka Hakes.
The legend of Michigan / written by Trinka Hakes Noble ;
illustrated by Gijsbert van Frankenhuyzen.
p. cm.
Summary: An old warrior and a young boy travel through the frigid cold of the north to teach the fierce North Wind how to live peacefully with his brothers, allowing the formerly uninhabitable land of Michigane to be settled.
ISBN 1-58536-278-6
[1. Winds—Fiction. 2. Cold—Fiction. 3. Indians of North America—Michigan—Fiction. 4. Michigan—Fiction.] I. Frankenhuyzen, Gijsbert van, ill. II. Title.
PZ7.N6715Leg 2006
[E]—dc22   2005027974

About The Legend of Michigan

The inspiration for *The Legend of Michigan* was drawn from my deep Michigan roots. I grew up on a farm near the Old Sauk Trail in southern Michigan, now called U.S. 12, which runs between Detroit and Chicago. Through my research I learned that this historic route marked the southern edge of the glacier that covered Michigan during the last Ice Age and was used by ancient Paleo-Indian peoples to skirt below the massive ice in their east/west travels. The topography along U.S. 12 vividly displays the glacier's effects, especially throughout the Irish Hills region and the rolling hills and farmland further west. South of U.S. 12, untouched by the glacier, the land flattens out.

Further research uncovered another ancient trail coming up from the south and connecting with the Sauk Trail about midway between Detroit and Lake Michigan. It was called the Old Maumee Trail.

After studying numerous creation myths and primitive legends overlapping the four seasons, winds, and directions, my writer's mind imagined the point where these two trails intersected to be the center of my hometown of Jonesville, on the corner of Maumee Street and U.S. 12, a short distance from the St. Joseph River. Native American lore and legend abound in this rural southern Michigan area and my childhood memories are filled with rich Potawatomi tales. So I set this story where these two ancient trails meet. From there, if you turn and face north, all of Michigan spreads out before you.

—*Trinka Hakes Noble*

Long long ago, the ancient peoples of the forest gathered around their warm bright fires and told the tale of a time long past, when the land of Michigane was covered with thick heavy ice.

It was a time before rivers flowed, before trees grew tall, before the howl of the timber wolf and the flying arrows of wild geese pierced the big blue skies. It was a time even before the ancient peoples came to Michigane themselves. They called it the Long Night of the North Wind.

Nothing stood in the way of the fierce North Wind as he howled down from his icy lodge from North of Up North. His cruel gales locked the land of the North in bitter cold, keeping it all to himself.

The East Wind, singing softly, brought the sunrise with his gentle breezes, but the North Wind howled louder and drowned him out.

The West Wind, smelling sweetly of prairie grasses, sent a chinook to thaw the ice, but the North Wind turned a cold shoulder and sent it back.

The South Wind, whose steamy eyes were always trained on the North, sent a hot huff and puff now and then, but the North Wind stared him down with an icy glare.

"I am the strongest of all the winds," boasted the North Wind. "No one can stop me!"

So for thousands of years the North Wind stormed over the
land of the North, freezing everything in his path until nothing
remained but heavy ice miles deep. Its massive weight crushed
rocks, scooped out great wide basins, and dug long ravines as
it inched ever southward. Winter stayed the whole year
around, so nothing could live in Michigane.

But one day the North Wind caught the scent of an old man journeying from the land of the East and a young boy traveling from the land of the South.

"What? Who dares to approach my domain?" he roared with a gusty rage. But thousands of years is a long time to go without a visitor, so the curious North Wind crept to the edge of his ice fields to listen as the two travelers met on the Old North Way.

The Old Warrior spoke first. "Little Warrior," he said to the boy as the bitter wind nipped at their heels, "what brings you to this cold and barren place?"

The boy addressed the Old Warrior with respect.

"Grandfather," he answered, "the North Wind has frozen every-thing. The fish are locked in ice. The deer have long vanished from our dying forest. My people are cold and hungry, and will perish soon. So I've come to ask the North Wind to be my brother and share his land of the North as a brother shares."

The North Wind lifted his snowy brow and scoffed to himself. "A brother! Who needs a little brother?"

"And you, Grandfather," questioned the boy, "how strange
to see such an old warrior so far from his fire."

For a moment the Old Warrior worried that his disguise had
failed him, for he really was the Great Spirit, the Gitche Manitou,
mighty creator of all. He had come to punish the North Wind,
but was touched by the boy's words.

So the cunning Gitche Manitou stooped lower in
his fur robe and pretended to shiver from the cold,
then spoke in a feeble voice.

"And that is why I am so glad our trails met, Little
Warrior. You are young and pure of heart. I am old
but have the wisdom of many winters. With your
good heart and my wisdom, perhaps we can mend
the harsh ways of the North Wind."

So the two journeyed together along the Old
North Way toward the place of the tall ice.

"Humph!" snorted the North Wind.
"They'll never last the night."

When darkness fell, the two camped on a snowy ridge. By now the boy was very cold.

"Grandfather," he shivered, "we have no fire."

The Gitche Manitou reached inside his fur travel bundle and produced a handful of dry sticks and built a little fire for the boy.

"Oh Grandfather, how wise to bring firewood!" exclaimed the boy as he clapped his mittened hands. The Gitche Manitou smiled back as wisps of smoke curled up into the vast northern night.

But the North Wind caught the smell of wood smoke and swooped down, for he had not seen a fire in thousands of years.

"What? They dare light a fire in my domain?" he hissed in jealous anger. "Humph! I'll show them fire!"

Suddenly streaks of light began to flash and flare across the northern horizon, then soared high into a shower of shimmering light—greens and yellows, pinks and blues—arching and dancing across the dark heavens like the glinting spears of many tribes. The boy jumped to his feet in wonder.

"Oh wise Grandfather, what is this I see above me?"

"It is the North Wind's Fire Lights," answered the Gitche Manitou. "The North Wind is showing off his powerful sky fire."

The boy was drawn to the lights like a magnet. He raced to the highest point on the ridge, spread out his arms and twirled.

"It is the North Wind inviting me to dance with him. Surely he wants to be my brother," laughed the boy with uplifted heart.

The North Wind was displeased that the boy did not fear his sky fire. No one had danced in his domain for thousands of years, so he sent more and more shimmering spears of light fanning out across the night sky until they nearly surrounded the Little Warrior, but the boy danced on.

The Gitche Manitou watched in silence for he did not trust the North Wind. "Tomorrow we reach the place of the tall ice," he mused under his breath. "Then we'll see if the North Wind can change his ways."

But the next morning, the North Wind was up to his old tricks. Relentlessly, he sent freezing sleet beating down on their camp, sealing everything in dazzling ice.

The Little Warrior awoke hungry and thirsty. "Oh Grandfather, what will we do?"

The mighty Gitche Manitou again reached inside his travel bundle and produced a supple gray twig. Instantly, it was coated with ice. "Here, let this melt slowly in your mouth."

The boy smiled, for the ice tasted faintly of sweet maple. "The North Wind has made ice candy for me. Surely he wants to be my brother," beamed the boy as they continued their journey.

This made the North Wind furious, so he doubled back on the trail and faced them with a full force gale so frigid that the boy's feet froze like stumps as he struggled to walk.

"Climb onto my back," said the Gitche Manitou. "I will carry you the rest of the way."

"Then let me give you one of my mittens," offered the boy as he handed the Gitche Manitou his left mitten and scrambled up on his back.

The Gitche Manitou marveled at the mitten's warmth. "Tell me of these mittens, Little Warrior," asked the Great Spirit as the two journeyed on.

"They are double deerskin mittens," began the Little Warrior. "Many Grandmothers before my Grandmother made these mittens from the last of the deer hunted by many Grandfathers before my Grandfather. And when there was no sinew left for repairs," continued the boy, "my Grandmother sewed them together with her silver hair. They are the last double deerskin mittens of my people."

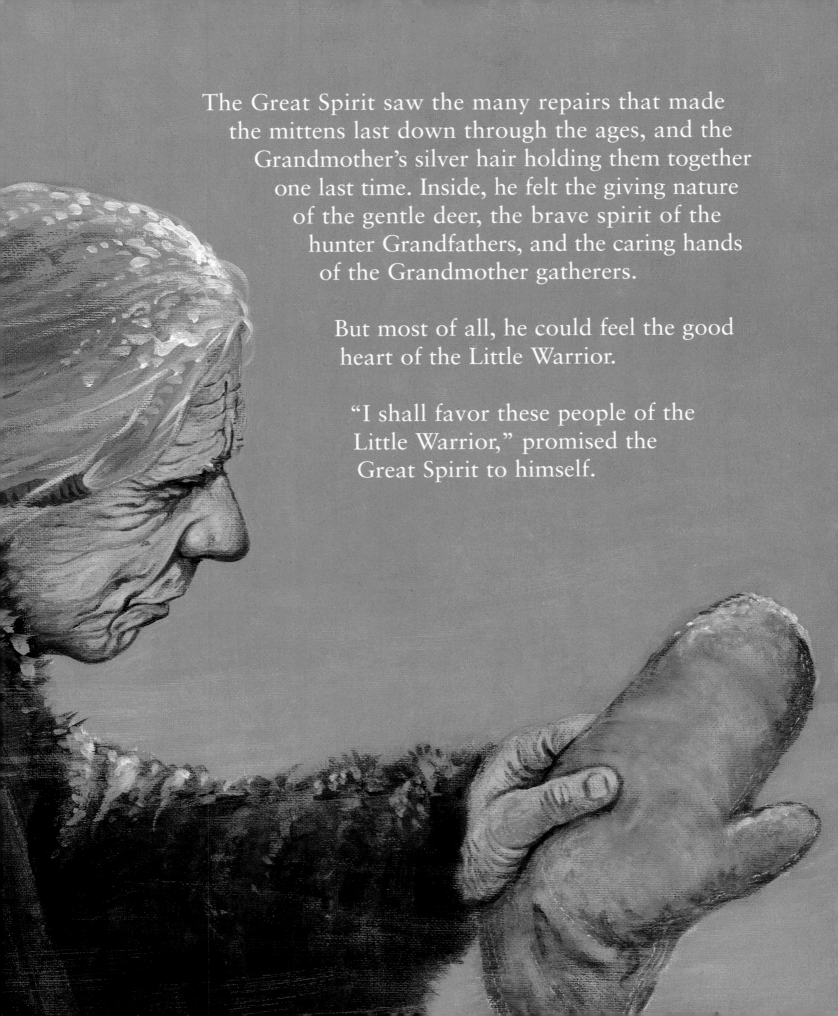

The Great Spirit saw the many repairs that made
the mittens last down through the ages, and the
Grandmother's silver hair holding them together
one last time. Inside, he felt the giving nature
of the gentle deer, the brave spirit of the
hunter Grandfathers, and the caring hands
of the Grandmother gatherers.

But most of all, he could feel the good
heart of the Little Warrior.

"I shall favor these people of the
Little Warrior," promised the
Great Spirit to himself.

When the two reached the place of the tall ice, the North Wind was outraged to see them at his front gate. He blasted forth such a powerful blizzard that even the Gitche Manitou had to squint, so the Little Warrior shielded the Gitche Manitou's eyes with his one mittened hand.

Then the Gitche Manitou raised his own mittened hand against the North Wind and demanded, "Stop! It is time for you to share as a brother shares!"

"What?" bellowed the North Wind. "You dare hold up two mere mittens against me?"

But the mighty Gitche Manitou had made the mittens more powerful, so blow as he might, the North Wind could not pierce the double deerskin mittens. Again and again he tried, shrieking and howling, but the Gitche Manitou and the Little Warrior kept their mittens in place until the North Wind had blown himself out.

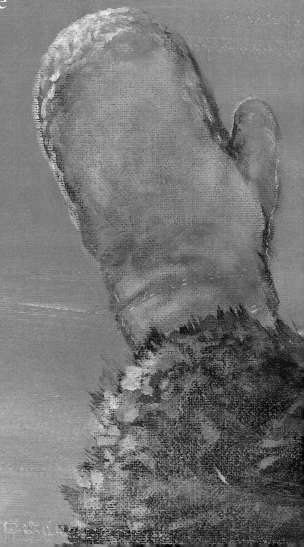

"Oh no," gasped the North Wind with suspicion as he began to lose his icy grip. "The Great Spirit must have a hand in this!"

Fearful of losing everything, the North Wind began to bargain with the Great Spirit. "If I agree to your demand," he sputtered, "what do I get in return?"

"For three moons each year your cold winds can rule the land," said the Great Spirit.

"Only three months? That's all I get?" whined the North Wind as he grew weaker.

So the Great Spirit sweetened the deal, for it was part of his plan all along.

"After the South Wind has sent his last warm puff called Indian Summer, your frosty winds can paint the leaves of the trees bright red, deep orange, and golden yellow. This will tell the people to harvest and store their crops and gather firewood for your coming. Then you can turn the land white with your snows, but the pines will remain green as a reminder of our agreement."

The North Wind fluttered with excitement at all the colors and thought a little green would go well with his white, so he wistfully agreed. Then he sighed, "When must I leave?"

"The West Wind will send his warm chinook as a messenger to thaw your ice so your brother the East Wind can sing his gentle songs of spring."

The North Wind began to warm to the idea but hesitated. "What about my sky fire?"

"The Northern Lights shall always be your domain," nodded the Great Spirit, "and at night the deer will stop their browse to admire you, and the moose will lift their heads from the rivers, and the timber wolves will serenade you."

"And my people will come from their villages," added the Little Warrior, "to gaze in wonder at your dancing spears of light."

"And will the children dance for me?"
whispered the North Wind with fading breath.

"Oh yes, brother North Wind, all the children
will dance," promised the Little Warrior.

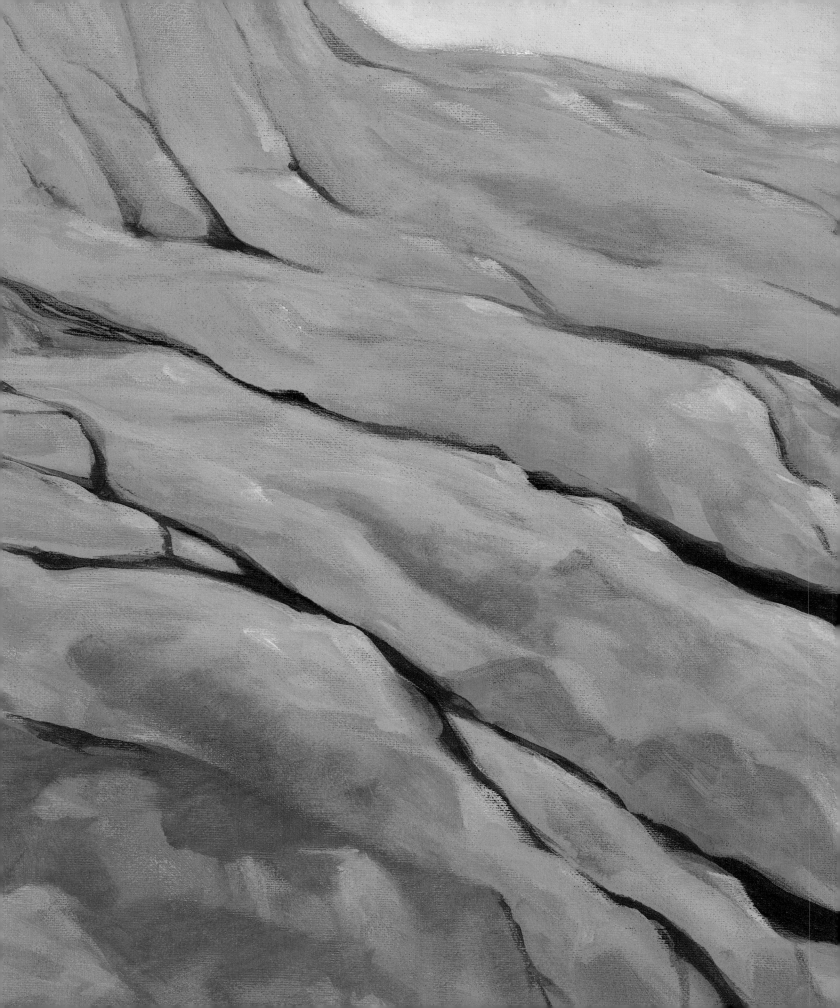

So the North Wind agreed to share as a brother shares, and retreated back to his icy lodge, North of Up North. The tall ice continued to melt until it set rivers flowing, filled all lakes, big and small, and surrounded the land of Michigane with deep great lakes of sparkling blue waters.

Then the West Wind, smelling sweetly, sent his seeds to blanket the land with prairie grasses, wild rice and oats and clover, then strew it all with wildflowers.

Now the East Wind, singing softly, sent the seeds from his ancient forests; maple, beech, and black walnut; sycamore, sassafras, and sumac too; sent his oaks to prairie openings, his great pines and spruces to the North and sprinkled in the birch and aspen.

And the South Wind, with his hot breath, sent his fruit trees, plum and cherry, sent the grape vines and wild berries, sent the squash, beans, and pumpkins to the land of Michigane.

And the Great Spirit kept his promise, favoring the
land of the Great Lakes, favoring this place where
the land lies pretty, favoring the land of Michigane.

But if the Long Night of the North Wind should ever return, the Great Spirit left his double deerskin mitten upon the land.

And the Little Warrior's mitten remains across the top as well, ever shielding the land of Michigan against the cold North Wind.

Trinka Hakes Noble

Trinka Hakes Noble is the noted author of numerous award-winning picture books including *The Scarlet Stockings Spy*, an IRA Teacher's Choice 2005, illustrated by Robert Papp. Ms. Noble also wrote the ever-popular *Jimmy's Boa* series and *Meanwhile Back at the Ranch*. Her many awards include ALA Notable Children's Book, *Booklist* Children's Editors' Choice, IRA-CBC Children's Choice, *Learning:* The Year's Ten Best, and several Junior Literary Guild Selections.

After graduating from Michigan State University as a fine arts major, Ms. Noble studied children's book writing and illustrating in New York City at Parsons School of Design, the New School University, Caldecott medalist Uri Shulevitz's Greenwich Village Workshop, and at New York University. A member of the Rutgers University Council on Children's Literature, she was awarded Outstanding Woman 2002 in Arts and Letters in the state of New Jersey for her lifetime work in children's books. Born and raised in Michigan, she currently lives with her husband in the historic Jockey Hollow area of Bernardsville, New Jersey. *The Legend of Michigan* is Ms. Noble's third book with Sleeping Bear Press.

Gijsbert van Frankenhuyzen

Artist Gijsbert van Frankenhuyzen knew from the age of ten that he wanted to be a children's book illustrator: Now, with over 20 books to his credit, he says he has loved every minute and brush stroke spent working on each one. In addition to *The Legend of Michigan*, Gijsbert's other picture books with Sleeping Bear Press include the bestselling *The Legend of Sleeping Bear*, *Mercedes and the Chocolate Pilot*, *Friend on Freedom River*, and his popular Hazel Ridge Farm stories, *Adopted by an Owl*, *Saving Samantha*, and *Kelly of Hazel Ridge*.

Gijsbert gets much of his inspiration from Hazel Ridge Farm, located in Bath, Michigan, where he lives with his wife, Robbyn. They both travel to schools in the Great Lakes area to share their love of wildlife through their art, writing, and storytelling. Visit their farm online at http://my.voyager.net/robbyn